P9-BZC-673

A Surprise Find

by Erin Falligant

illustrated by Arcana Studios

⭐ American Girl®

Questions or comments? Call 1-800-845-0005, visit our Web site at
americangirl.com, or write to Customer Service, American Girl,
8400 Fairway Place, Middleton, WI 53562-0497.

Printed in China
11 12 13 14 15 16 LEO 10 9 8 7 6 5 4 3 2 1

All American Girl and Innerstar University marks and Amber™, Emmy™,
Isabel™, Logan™, Neely™, Paige™, Riley™, and Shelby™ are trademarks
of American Girl, LLC.

Illustrations by Thu Thai at Arcana Studios

Cataloging-in-Publication Data available from the Library of Congress

INNERSTARU.com

Welcome to Innerstar University! At this imaginary, one-of-a-kind school, you can live with your friends in a dorm called Brightstar House and find lots of fun ways to let your true talents shine. Your friends at Innerstar U will help you find your way through some challenging situations, too.

When you reach a page in this book that asks you to make a decision, choose carefully. The decisions you make will lead to more than 20 different endings! (*Hint:* Use a pencil to check off your choices. That way, you'll never read the same story twice.)

Want to try another ending? Read the book again—and then again. Find out what would have happened if you'd made *different* choices. Then head to www.innerstarU.com for even more book endings, games, and fun with friends.

Innerstar Guides

Every girl needs a few good friends to help her find her way. These are the friends who are always there for **you.**

Emmy

A brave girl who loves swimming and boating

Isabel

A confident girl with a funky sense of style

Riley

A good sport, on the field and off

Paige

A nature lover who leads hikes and campus cleanups

Amber

An animal lover and
a loyal friend

Neely

A creative girl who loves
dance, music, and art

Logan

A super-smart girl
who is curious about
EVERYTHING

Shelby

A kind girl who is there
for her friends—and loves
making NEW friends!

Innerstar U Campus

1. Rising Star Stables
2. Star Student Center
3. Brightstar House
4. Starlight Library
5. Sparkle Studios
6. Blue Sky Nature Center

7. Real Spirit Center
8. Five-Points Plaza
9. Starfire Lake & Boathouse
10. U-Shine Hall

11. Good Sports Center
12. Shopping Square
13. The Market
14. Morningstar Meadow

ou check your watch for the third time in the past fifteen minutes. Isabel is going to be here any second to pick up your donations for Innerstar University's "Care and Share" clothing drive. You glance at your nearly empty donation box and start to panic.

It's just so hard to part with your things! Everything you own reminds you of someone or something, like the blue T-shirt you wore your first day here at Innerstar U. You wore a matching bracelet, too—a gift from Olivia, your best friend from back home. You haven't worn that bracelet in forever. Do you still have it?

You set down your donation box and open the bottom drawer of your jewelry box. There it is—a row of blue glass beads strung onto a braided green cord. Olivia made one just like it for herself. Looking at the bracelet makes you really miss her. When you hear a knock on your door, you sigh and drop the bracelet back into the jewelry box.

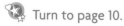 Turn to page 10.

You open your door, and Isabel bursts into your room, a red-headed whirlwind of energy and excitement. She's been looking forward to this clothing drive for weeks now. Neely trails behind Isabel, lugging a couple of brown grocery bags filled with clothing.

"Hey!" says Isabel. "Did you find things to donate?" She sees the box in your closet and bounds over to take a look. She lifts the box and shakes it a little. "Is this it?" she asks, looking up at you with a shocked expression.

"Yeah," you say, staring at your stocking feet. "I guess I don't have very much to give away."

Isabel kneels beside the pile of clothes on your floor— all the things you tried on and then decided you couldn't part with. "What about these?" she asks, picking up a pair of jeans with rhinestones on the pockets. She holds up the jeans to check the length. They're clearly way too short.

"I was thinking about turning them into capri pants," you mumble, yanking the jeans out of Isabel's hands.

Neely reaches out to touch the rhinestones on the pockets. "I could show you how to turn those pockets into a purse," she says. "They're much too pretty to give away."

"Neely, don't encourage her!" Isabel teases, and Neely raises her hands apologetically. She can't help it—she's always coming up with creative ideas, and now she has *you* thinking about that rhinestone purse, too.

 Turn to page 12.

Isabel pokes through your pile of clothes and makes a few more attempts to add to your box. "How about the fringed shorts?" she asks.

You shake your head no.

"These neon orange sneakers?"

Nope.

"The purple frog pajamas?"

Definitely not. "I'm sorry, Isabel," you say. "I want to help out with the clothing drive, but this is really hard."

Isabel's shoulders slump, but not for long. "Well," she says as she jumps up and brushes off her skirt, "you can always donate your *time*. We need people to help sort the clothes that come in. We're going to give some of the clothes to Casual Closet. The store is opening a secondhand shop in its basement to raise money for charity. Do you want to help sort clothes?"

Perfect! You're about to seize the opportunity when Neely pipes up. "Or . . . ," she says thoughtfully, her blue eyes shining, "you could help me make jewelry. We're going to sell it and then donate the money we raise."

You pause, mouth open. Both ideas sound good to you. Which do you choose?

 If you decide to help make jewelry, turn to page 14.

 If you decide to help sort clothes, turn to page 16.

You head back across campus toward Brightstar House, mentally sorting your closet as you walk. You have a couple of sweaters from Aunt Jess that could definitely go. They're nice and new but not really your style. One of them still has a store tag on it.

You also have two of the same striped shirt—a funny accident from last year when Shelby bought you a shirt for your birthday that you already had. The thought fills you with a rush of warmth. Shelby is a great friend who really knows your style. You never told her about the twin shirts because you didn't want to hurt her feelings, but after talking with her today, you don't think she'll mind if you donate one of the striped shirts.

 Turn to page 21.

Neely's enthusiasm for all things crafty is contagious. You agree to help her—and you start by offering to carry one of her bags of clothing. As you follow Neely and Isabel along the path toward the Market, you shift the bag of clothing from arm to arm. It's a long walk, and you're more than ready to set the bag down by the time you reach the cluster of bright donation tents.

Beneath the yellow awning of a tiny tent, a few girls are sitting at a table, stringing beads onto cord. A rack of finished necklaces is perched on the table.

"Ooh," you say, picking up a beaded necklace and admiring the handiwork. "Who made this one?"

"I did," says Neely with a hint of pride in her voice. "Want me to show you how?"

You nod and sit down across from Neely. She teaches you a few jewelry-making tricks, and before you know it, an hour has gone by.

When the rack of jewelry starts to overflow, Neely sets up a selling stand just outside the tent. Unfortunately, when she leaves the table, your creativity starts to fade. You glance around, searching for inspiration.

You suddenly think of your bracelet from Olivia and how she cleverly knotted the cord in between beads to keep them secure. You decide to run back to your room to get the bracelet to show the other girls.

Turn to page 18.

You decide to sort clothes, hoping that it'll make up for the *lack* of clothes in your own donation box. You follow Isabel to the donation tents at the Market, where volunteers have already begun sorting clothing into piles.

"Hey!" calls your good friend Shelby. "Over here!" She and another friend, Amber, are sorting shirts. They make room for you to stand at the table beside them.

The three of you separate the shirts into two boxes: a "donate" box and a "recycle into rags" box. Unfortunately, the "rags" box is nearly overflowing. Lots of the clothing is too dirty or beat-up to donate.

"I can't believe someone would give us this," says Shelby, holding up a T-shirt with a huge purple stain on the front. "We should be donating only the things that *we* would want to wear."

Shelby is right. She's generous that way. In fact, she's the girl who really *would* give the shirt off her back to a friend in need.

Turn to page 19.

When you get back to your room, you head straight to your closet to grab the bracelet out of your jewelry box. You pull open the drawer and find . . . nothing. The drawer is empty.

You search your closet shelves. No bracelet. You pick up the piles of clothes on your floor and search the rug beneath. No bracelet.

Now you're starting to panic. You retrace the events of the morning: You were sorting clothes and had managed to put one or two things into the donation box. You set it down to look for your bracelet. You heard a knock on your door. You put your bracelet back into your jewelry box. *Uh-oh.* Could the bracelet have accidentally fallen into the donation box?

Turn to page 20.

Listening to Shelby talk, you feel a pang of guilt. Surely you could have found more clothes in your closet to donate this morning. Why is it so hard for you to part with things? Maybe your friends can help you figure that out.

"Hey, how did you guys decide what to donate?" you ask Shelby and Amber while you work.

Amber grins. "That was easy," she says. "I'd just hold up a piece of clothing and ask myself, 'If a dog ate this, would I have to run right out and get another one?' If the answer was no, that thing went into the donate pile."

Shelby giggles and shakes her head. You laugh, too. Amber is all about dogs, dogs, dogs, but her sorting method is a good one. Will it work for you? Maybe. You decide to give it a try.

You sort a few more shirts with Shelby and Amber, but when they take a snack break, you tell them that you're going to run back to your room for a bit.

Turn to page 13.

You race back to the donation tents looking for Isabel. "She's not here," Neely tells you. "She's bringing some of the sorted clothes to Casual Closet."

That's okay, you tell yourself. Surely your bracelet is here somewhere in the donated piles. It couldn't be too deeply buried, could it? You just brought your things here a couple of hours ago.

You're about to start digging through donations when Neely asks, "Can you take my place at the jewelry-selling stand for a minute? I need to run to my room to get more beads and cord. The more jewelry we make, the more we'll sell—and the more money we can bring in today!"

You think about telling Neely about your lost bracelet, but she's obviously too caught up in the jewelry sale right now. You would be, too, if you weren't so worried about your bracelet.

If you tell Neely that you don't have time to help right now, turn to page 22.

If you agree to take Neely's place at the jewelry-selling stand, turn to page 48.

When you get to your room, you grab some paper bags from your closet. The first thing that goes into a bag is those rhinestone jeans. Neely could help you cut them apart to make a purse, but it'd be better to give them to a girl who will actually wear them (a girl who is a couple of inches shorter than you!).

You fill the bags with more clothes, including that blue T-shirt from your first day of classes a year ago. You haven't worn it in months. Sure, it makes you think of Olivia, but you'll always have the bracelet from her. You'll keep that instead.

You suddenly realize that you never put the bracelet away this morning. Where did you leave it? You search your jewelry box and the shelves nearby. After looking for a few minutes, you give up. You'll find the bracelet later. Right now, you need to get back to the donation tents.

 Turn to page 25.

"I'm sorry," you call to Neely over your shoulder. "There's something I have to do before I can help with the sale." You *have* to find that bracelet. But where do you start?

You head for a stack of cardboard boxes. Is one of the boxes yours? You start unstacking the boxes until you reach one that looks sort of familiar. The clothes inside don't, but maybe your things are at the bottom. You dump the clothes onto the ground and start digging through them.

"Hey, what are you doing?" asks one of the volunteers. It's Kayla, or is her name Kailey? You can't remember. She's new at Innerstar U. She has long golden hair and freckles, which are popping right now against her pink cheeks. She looks annoyed.

"I lost something," you explain hurriedly. "I think it must be in one of these boxes."

"Okay," she says. "But take it easy on the clothes. If you get those dirty, we won't be able to donate them."

You don't appreciate the scolding, but the girl does have a point. You carefully put the clothes back into the box and begin searching through another.

🐾 Turn to page 24.

You search the entire stack of boxes, but you don't find what you're looking for. You also check with the girls who are sorting clothes in a nearby tent. None of them have seen your bracelet.

Isabel may be your only hope. You half-walk, half-run across the grassy field toward Shopping Square. Casual Closet is at the far end of the shopping center, which seems like miles away. When you finally reach the shop, you burst through the front doors and then skip down the stairs to the basement. You dodge a few clothing racks and head toward the back room, where you find Isabel and a couple of other volunteers hanging clothes on racks.

"Isabel," you say, trying to catch your breath, "have you seen my bracelet? Blue beads . . . green cord. It might have gotten mixed up in my donations this morning."

Isabel shakes her head distractedly. But after a moment, your question registers. She pauses, a shirt hanger in hand, and glances up at you. "Wait," she says. "I think I *did* see that. It was on the floor of your closet by your donation box. I put it in the box. I thought you were giving it away!"

Isabel is horrified, but you're relieved. At least you know what happened to the bracelet. Next question: Where is it *now*?

 Turn to page 26.

When you get back to the tents, you find Amber sorting shirts all by herself. "Shelby had to run to the yearbook office," explains Amber. "When she gets back, you and I can go to lunch, if you want."

"Sounds good," you say. "Sorry I took so long. I brought a few things to add to the pile."

As you pull your clothes out of the paper bags, you tell Amber about your missing bracelet. "I hope I didn't really lose it," you say, "because there are so many memories tied to it."

Amber nods thoughtfully and then says, "Maybe it's time to make some *new* ones. You should invite Olivia to Innerstar U for a visit. I'd like to meet her."

Great idea! you think. Olivia came to visit you last year, but that was before you really knew Amber and lots of your other friends. You make up your mind to e-mail Olivia right away. The more you think about it, the more excited you get.

When Shelby returns, Amber finishes taping a box shut and then asks, "Ready to go to lunch?" You hesitate. You can't decide whether to go straight to lunch or to stop at your room first to e-mail Olivia.

If you stop at your room, turn to page 27.

If you go straight to lunch, turn to page 28.

Isabel wants to help you find the bracelet, but she points to the box of clothes at her feet. "Can you help?" she asks. "We'll get through this more quickly if you do."

You agree to sort clothes. It's hard at first to concentrate, but you finally get into the rhythm of sorting. Pretty soon you've filled a rack with skirts in all kinds of styles and colors. Isabel is enjoying the work, too. Creating displays of pretty clothes is right up her alley.

The owner of Casual Closet thanks you for your hard work and asks if you're free to come back this afternoon. The clothing room opens to the public tomorrow, and she's hoping to have all donations on display by then.

If you agree to come back to help, turn to page 29.

If you say that you have other plans (like searching for your bracelet), turn to page 30.

"I'll meet you in the cafeteria," you tell Amber. "I just need to stop at my room first."

Amber walks you all the way to Brightstar House, and then she continues on the stone path toward the student center. You take the steps to your room two at a time and head straight for your computer. The first thing you do is pull up Olivia's family blog. She used to update it all the time so that you could keep track of what she was doing, but it looks as if she hasn't posted anything new in weeks.

You decide to e-mail Olivia a short note, but that note quickly turns into a long letter. It feels good to "talk" with your old friend. You tell her all about the Care and Share clothing drive. You almost tell her about your hunt for the lost bracelet this morning, but you don't. You've convinced yourself that it'll turn up soon—which means it's not really lost, right?

You hit "send" and then take off for the student center, hoping you're not too late to meet Amber for lunch.

 Turn to page 31.

You're pretty hungry and don't want to leave Amber hanging, so you decide to go straight to lunch with her. You can always e-mail Olivia later.

As you walk the winding path across campus, Amber asks you if you've checked the Lost and Found for your missing bracelet.

"The Lost and Found?" you ask. "Where's that?"

"At the student center," says Amber. "Haven't you ever been there? It's where they keep things like lost sunglasses and cell phones. I accidentally left my backpack in a tent at the Market once, and it turned up at the Lost and Found."

Hmm. You think it's a long shot that your bracelet will be at the Lost and Found. It's probably still back in your room somewhere. But as you step into the student center, Amber points down the hall past the bakery. "It's right down there," she says. "Should we just check?"

 If you check the Lost and Found, turn to page 41.

 If you go straight to the cafeteria to satisfy your hungry stomach, turn to page 59.

You agree to come back to Casual Closet after lunch. Sorting clothes and creating displays helped take your mind off your bracelet. You'll do a quick search for it over the noon hour, but if it doesn't turn up, you'll let it go—at least for now.

You run to the Star Student Center with Isabel to buy sandwiches for yourselves and the other volunteers. When you get back to the donation tents, you turn them upside down looking for the bracelet. No luck.

You can tell that Isabel feels awful. She peeks at you from behind her glasses. "I'm so sorry," she says. "I'd make you another bracelet, but I know it wouldn't be the same."

"It's okay," you tell her. And really, it is. It's time to get back to Casual Closet, and you're feeling pretty excited about preparing the secondhand shop for its grand opening tomorrow. You throw your arm around Isabel's shoulders and walk with her to the shop.

You spend the afternoon organizing jeans by size and hanging them on a long rack. When you're all done, you're proud of your work. The rack looks great! When the owner of Casual Closet invites you to tomorrow's grand opening, you give her a hearty yes.

Turn to page 70.

You feel great about what you accomplished at Casual Closet, but you're ready to get back to your search for the bracelet. Isabel follows you to the donation tents. You do some more digging, but the bracelet is nowhere to be found. You leave for lunch feeling totally discouraged.

You load up a food tray at the student center and sit down with Isabel and your friend Paige. During lunch, all you can talk about is your bracelet. As you describe it to Paige, she gets a strange look on her freckled face.

"I *just* saw one like that," Paige says. "I was in line behind that new girl, Kayla, and I noticed her bracelet. The beads were as blue as the sky." Paige falls silent.

Did Kayla find the bracelet and decide to keep it for herself? That'd be a pretty rotten thing to do, especially after she saw you searching so frantically for the bracelet. *She didn't know what you were searching for,* you remind yourself. But still, you can't help feeling a little angry.

You scan the lunchroom looking for Kayla. There she is—sitting alone at a table. It looks as if she has finished eating and is getting ready to leave.

"Just remember that the bracelet might not be yours," Isabel cautions you. Paige looks worried, too, as if she thinks she just got Kayla into big trouble.

 If you follow Kayla out of the room, turn to page 32.

 If you ask Kayla straight-out about the bracelet, turn to page 64.

When you get to the cafeteria, you scan the tables full of girls, searching for Amber's black braids. You check your watch: 12:58. You had no idea how late it was! Amber must have already gone back to the Market.

You grab a sandwich and then hurry back to the tents. You're relieved to find Amber there, sitting beside Shelby and a pile of folded shirts. A striped sleeve hangs out of the otherwise tidy pile in front of Amber. It's the shirt you donated this morning. *Uh-oh.* You never had time to explain to Shelby why you gave the shirt away. You quickly tuck the shirtsleeve into the pile, hoping Shelby hasn't seen it.

"Hey!" Amber says to you. "We have lots of volunteers here this afternoon. You can duck out if you need to."

You don't really *need* to, but you're eager to watch your e-mail to see if Olivia writes you back. When you get to your room, you're thrilled to see that she has!

> **From:** Olivia
> **CC:**
> **REPLY** **Subject:** A visit!
>
> I'd LOVE to come for a visit! My mom is traveling for business next Sunday and is going right by Innerstar U. She says she can drop me off for the day. Hooray! I can't WAIT to see you.
> Livvy

 Turn to page 34.

You follow Kayla out of the lunchroom, with Paige and Isabel close behind. Isabel is whispering something to you. She clearly doesn't think this is a good idea. When she grabs your hand to slow you down, you pull it away and end up elbowing Paige, who squeals in surprise. Kayla glances over her shoulder, and you drop to your knee, pretending to tie your shoe.

Kayla stops at the Sweet Treats bakery. You get in line, too, behind Becca, a girl you know from soccer. When Kayla reaches out to pay for her cookie, you strain to see her wrist—and you accidentally step on Becca's heels.

"Hey, watch out!" Becca says, sliding her foot back into her shoe.

Kayla looks backward and gives you a puzzled look. As she turns to walk away, someone calls your name. It's your friend Logan, who sometimes helps out at the bakery. She's standing behind the counter.

"What's going on?" Logan asks. "Why are you acting so weird?"

Weird? Leave it to Logan to pick right up on whatever's going on with you.

If you tell Logan that you think Kayla has your bracelet, turn to page 35.

If you ignore Logan's question and follow Kayla out the door, turn to page 38.

Olivia is coming on Sunday—just a week from now! You tell your friends about her upcoming visit at dinner, and they're almost as excited about it as you are.

"I can't wait to meet her!" says Amber. "Maybe you can bring her to the stables. Does she like to ride horses?"

"I'll bet she's crafty, like you," says Neely. "We could hang out at the art studio—that'd be fun."

"Or the Market," says Isabel. "Does she like to shop?"

You appreciate your friends' enthusiasm, but you're starting to get worried. Back home, you and Olivia were two peas in a pod—always together, just the two of you. She was your best friend, but you've met so many new friends here at Innerstar U. Will Olivia want to hang out with them? Will she feel left out—or worse yet, replaced?

When Sunday comes, you try to push your worries out of your mind. *Everything will work out*, you tell yourself. *Just focus on having fun with your old friend.*

You wait for Olivia at the student center. When she walks through the door, your heart leaps. She's taller and is wearing her hair in a different style, but one look at her smile tells you that it's the same old Olivia. You run to her and pull her into a big hug.

Olivia's mom gives you a hug, too, and says she'll pick up Olivia after dinner. Then you and Olivia link arms and start walking back to Brightstar House.

Turn to page 36.

You step closer to the counter so that you can tell Logan what's going on. "I think Kayla took my bracelet," you whisper—apparently too loudly, because Becca turns around and asks, "Who stole what?"

Isabel pipes up from behind you and says, "Nobody *stole* anything."

"Okay, maybe she didn't steal it," you say, "but she has it, and I need to get it back."

"You don't *know* that she has it," Paige adds softly. "Just remember that, okay?" She gives you a pleading look.

"Sounds like a real mystery," says Logan. She starts to launch into a detailed account of a mystery book she's been reading, but you don't have time to listen. You've got to figure out which way Kayla went.

Turn to page 39.

You've barely taken ten steps before you run into Amber and Shelby, who are on their way to Rising Star Stables. "Perfect timing!" says Amber. "Do you want to come riding with us?"

You look at Olivia, who is smiling shyly at your friends. You can't tell by her expression whether she wants to go riding or not. Would she rather spend some one-on-one time with you?

You hesitate. "It'd be fun to go riding," you tell Amber, "but Olivia just got here. We have to talk and figure out what we're going to do first."

Amber shrugs good-naturedly and says, "No worries. If you decide you want to ride, come find us!"

Turn to page 40.

You follow Kayla along the path between the student center and the library. As you cross the footbridge behind her, Kayla glances over her shoulder. You stop walking and lean over the rail, pretending to be enjoying the view of the stream.

When you turn back around, you see Kayla climbing the front steps to the library and pulling open the front door. A few seconds later, you step through that same door, but you don't see Kayla anywhere. How did she disappear so quickly?

You scan the stacks of books and all of the reading chairs along the windows. Then you climb the long flight of stairs to the reading room that overlooks campus on three sides and the library courtyard on the other. You press your nose up against the window, searching the courtyard below. There she is! Kayla is sitting on a bench beneath a tree, reading a book.

 Turn to page 44.

You push your way through a crowd of girls. Did Kayla go out the front door of the student center? You're not sure. You run out the door and onto the front patio, scanning the steps and paths beyond in search of Kayla's blonde hair. There's no sign of her.

Becca steps out onto the patio beside you, carrying a half-eaten muffin. "Did you catch the thief?" she asks.

You hear Isabel's voice in your head saying, *Nobody stole anything.*

If you correct Becca, turn to page 43.

If you say nothing, turn to page 50.

Back in your room, Olivia wanders around, looking at your posters, stuffed animals, and other things. "This is so cool," she says. "Half of this stuff was in your old room and looks really familiar, and the other half is brand-new—and really fun!"

When Olivia stops to look at the photos on your vanity mirror, you feel a twinge of guilt. You should have put more pictures of her up there along with pictures of your new friends.

You feel even guiltier when Olivia reaches to fix her hair in the mirror and you see the bracelet on her wrist. It's the one she made that matches yours—or that matches the bracelet you *used* to have.

If you confess to Olivia that you might have lost the bracelet, turn to page 42.

If you stay quiet about the bracelet, turn to page 46.

When you get to the Lost and Found, you're amazed by everything you see behind the counter. There are boxes full of sweatshirts, jackets, T-shirts, hats, sunglasses, backpacks, and other items—but no bracelet.

The girl behind the counter seems as disappointed as you are that you didn't find what you were looking for. "More lost items come in than found items go out," she says. "It's really time to clear out some of this stuff."

You're about to walk away when an idea strikes. "Hey," you say, "maybe you could donate some of this to the clothing drive. That'd be a great way to get things out of here and into the hands of people who could use them."

The girl's eyes light up at the suggestion, but then her face falls. "We have to keep all of this for at least a month before giving it away," she says. "Just in case an owner comes to look for something. The problem is, we don't keep good track of what comes in when. It's a total mess."

While you're eating lunch, your mind keeps wandering back to that counter. You feel bad for all the girls who are missing their things and don't realize they're waiting to be picked up at the Lost and Found. On the other hand, you wish you could donate everything there to the clothing drive. Isabel would be ecstatic!

 Turn to page 63.

You hate telling Olivia that you lost the bracelet she made for you, but it's better than her thinking you just don't like it or don't want to wear it anymore.

"Livvy," you begin, "there's something I have to tell you."

Olivia's expression turns serious. She leans against the edge of your vanity, her eyes wide. "What is it?" she asks solemnly.

"It's about the bracelet you made me last year," you say, pointing to the one on Olivia's wrist. "I can't find it. I think I might have actually lost it." You hold your breath, waiting for her response.

Olivia glances at your bare wrist and then breaks into a grin. She looks as relieved as you suddenly feel. "Is that all?" she asks. "Then I have a confession of my own to make. I broke my bracelet a few months ago and had to make a new one. See?"

Olivia holds out her wrist. Sure enough, the band on this bracelet is slightly different. It's made out of green embroidery floss instead of cord.

"I can make *you* a new one, too," adds Olivia.

You instantly feel lighter. "Thanks!" you say. "I'd love that." Telling Olivia about the bracelet was the right call. With that conversation behind you, you're ready to get on with your day together.

Turn to page 47.

It pains you to say so, but you know Isabel is right. "We don't know for sure that Kayla took the bracelet," you tell Becca.

She raises an eyebrow. "But you *think* she did, right?" she asks. Becca loves a good drama.

"I'm just following her so that I can ask her about it," you say. That's not quite true. You don't think you'll be brave enough to ask Kayla outright about the bracelet, but you have to shut Becca down. You don't want her telling people that Kayla stole the bracelet unless you know for sure. And even then, this is between you and Kayla.

Becca's shoulders slump. She looks as if she's lost her passion for this "story," and that's a good thing.

As Becca heads back into the student center, you start down the path that leads to Starlight Library. The group of girls in front of you thins out a bit, and you suddenly catch a glimpse of the back of a blonde head. It's Kayla!

 Turn to page 38.

You scurry down the stairs, nearly tripping in your haste. You're afraid Kayla will leave before you get to her —she's proving to be a tough girl to track. But as you step into the courtyard, you see her there, still peacefully reading beneath the leafy branches of a large tree.

You tiptoe around the outer edge of the courtyard and find a bench on the other side of the tree. You sit down, carefully peering over your shoulder to see if you can catch a glimpse of Kayla's wrist. Wait, where'd she go? Kayla's gone, her book resting on the bench where she was sitting just a few seconds ago.

"Are you following me?" a voice asks.

You whirl around and see Kayla standing right in front of you. "No! What? Of course not," you say, stumbling over your words.

You wish you'd brought a book to read or homework to do—anything to make you look as if you belong here. You didn't, so instead, you stretch out on the bench and try to look comfortable. "I was just going to catch some ZZZs," you say as casually as you can.

It's hard to keep a casual expression on your face, though, when you catch sight of the bracelet peeking out from beneath Kayla's shirtsleeve. The cord of the bracelet is more turquoise than green. It's *not* yours.

Now what?

 Turn to page 52.

You try not to think about your missing bracelet, but you find yourself pulling your sleeves down with your hands to cover your bare wrists.

When Olivia's bracelet catches on a button on her skirt and she works to untangle it, you're sure she's going to ask you about your own bracelet—but she doesn't. After that, it's hard to concentrate on anything she's saying.

Olivia can tell that something's bugging you. She cocks her head. "Do you want to go meet up with your friends?" she asks. Maybe she thinks you're bored.

You hesitate. "We could," you say. "Is that what *you* want to do?"

Olivia shrugs. "Sure," she says. "That'd be fun."

You're relieved. Maybe hanging out with your friends will take your mind off the bracelet, and you'll be able to act more normal with Olivia. You don't want her to think that you're not having fun with her.

 Turn to page 60.

You pack a *lot* into the next couple of hours, hurrying Olivia from one activity to the next. There's so much you want to show her!

You skip rocks at the edge of the lake, listen to a band play onstage at the Market, and rent kites to fly in the meadow. Afterward, you walk through Five-Points Plaza so that you can throw coins into the fountain and make a wish. Your wish is that Olivia will come back for many more visits like this one. You can't tell her that, though— then your wish might not come true.

You're heading into Sparkle Studios to make some crafts when you run into Neely, who's just leaving.

"Hi!" she says. "I was going to get dinner. Do you two want to come?" She turns to Olivia and adds, "Everyone will be there. You can meet a bunch of our friends!"

Olivia bites her lip and looks at you. "Do you want to go?" she asks you.

You're not sure. The question is, *What does Olivia want to do?* You search her eyes for some sign. Given how long you two have been friends, you'd think you would have come up with a secret code for times like this—tugging on your ear means "yes," scratching your nose means "no," or *something*. You didn't, and now you're just left guessing.

 If you go with Neely to dinner, turn to page 58.

 If you tell Neely that you and Olivia want to make a few crafts first, turn to page 62.

You agree to watch the jewelry-selling stand. Neely has done so much for this fund-raiser. The least you can do is cover her spot for a few minutes.

You plunk down in the chair by the cash box. There is a lot of money in the box already. You're sorting the money when your friend Emmy walks by. She looks as if she's in a hurry to get somewhere—probably the lake, where she's a junior lifeguard. When she sees you, though, she changes direction and comes to say hello.

"Hey there! What're you doing?" Emmy asks.

As you're explaining the jewelry sale to her, Emmy fingers the necklaces and bracelets hanging off the display racks in front of you.

"Wow," she says, pulling a bracelet off the rack. "This one is beautiful. It reminds me of the lake."

You glance at the blue-beaded bracelet, which looks awfully familiar.

Just then, you hear a loud commotion behind you. It's Neely, carrying an armload of jewelry-making supplies. She must have dropped a bag of beads, because you can see a spray of them bouncing across the cobblestones.

 If you jump up to help Neely pick up the beads, turn to page 51.

 If you finish talking with Emmy first, turn to page 53.

You don't take the time to correct Becca. You just shake your head no and run down the path toward the Market. Maybe Kayla is heading back to the donation tents.

Nope—Kayla's not there. It's as if she left the bakery with her cookie and just walked off into the sunset. Too bad there isn't a trail of crumbs you could follow.

Neely finds you by the jewelry tent, staring into space. "Did you come to help make jewelry?" she asks brightly.

Not exactly, you think to yourself, but you can't tell Neely that. There's a fund-raiser going on here, which means there's no time to pout—or to scheme about ways to catch a bracelet stealer.

You do pout, though, as you're sitting at the craft table stringing beads onto cord. One of the other volunteers asks you what's wrong, and you tell her about your lost bracelet. You lovingly describe every detail, as if you're sure you'll never see it again.

"Why don't you just buy another one?" she asks you.

The question annoys you. "I can't," you tell her. "This was one-of-a-kind. There aren't any more like it."

"Sure there are," she says. "We made a bunch like that this morning. Go check the sales table."

You can't believe this girl—she's got a lot of nerve. But you can't hide your curiosity, either. After a moment of silence, you push your chair back dramatically and walk over to the stand where Neely is selling jewelry.

 Turn to page 54.

You leap out of your chair to help Neely pick up the beads before they all roll away. As you gather the smooth glass beads in your hands, you notice the rich swirls of color inside them. The beads remind you of marbles.

You're dreaming of the beautiful bracelets you'll create with these beads when you suddenly remember the bracelet Emmy was holding at the jewelry table. It looked an awful lot like yours—the one Olivia made for you.

As you toss a handful of beads into Neely's plastic bag, you glance back at the jewelry table. Emmy is gone. When you get back to the table, you see that something else is gone, too—the bracelet you think is yours. But there are a couple of dollars on the table beside the cash box. Emmy must have paid for the bracelet and taken it with her. *Now* what?

 If you wait a few minutes until Neely is settled back down at the jewelry-selling stand, turn to page 57.

 If you take off looking for Emmy—and your bracelet— turn to page 74.

You don't think Kayla bought your story. It doesn't help that as soon as she returns to her bench, you hop up from yours and hurry back toward the student center. You're hoping Isabel and Paige are still there.

You find your friends at the bakery, still talking with Logan. You approach them sheepishly, like a dog with her tail between her legs.

"Well?" asks Isabel. "Did you catch up with Kayla?"

You nod, but you can't quite meet Isabel's eyes. "You were right," you mumble. "She didn't have my bracelet."

Logan breaks the uncomfortable silence that follows. "Let's start at the beginning," she says. "Your bracelet got mixed up with some clothes in a donation box, right?"

"Right," you say. Clearly your friends have filled Logan in on things while you were away.

"You went to the donation tents to find the bracelet, and you searched through all the donated clothes, right?" Logan continues.

You nod.

"But why?" asks Logan. "Why search for jewelry in a pile of clothing? If I were searching for jewelry, I'd look for it in a pile of *jewelry*."

You're about to tell Logan that it was a clothing drive, not a jewelry drive. But then you remember Neely's jewelry-selling stand. Maybe Logan is on to something!

Turn to page 83.

You want to help Neely, but there's something about the bracelet in Emmy's hand that keeps you glued to your seat.

"I have to have this," says Emmy. "How much is it?" She holds out the bracelet for you to see. Now there's no mistaking it. That's *your* bracelet!

 If you let Emmy hold on to the bracelet for a moment, turn to page 66.

 If you grab the bracelet back and tell Emmy that it isn't for sale, turn to page 69.

Neely is making change for a customer at the sales table, which gives you a chance to look through the jewelry. Sure enough, there's a whole *rack* of blue-beaded bracelets for sale. You gasp and start flipping through them.

None of the bracelets is your special one from Olivia. You can tell because these are made with turquoise cord instead of green. Still, the bracelets are awfully good imitations of yours. How is that possible? Is the universe playing some cruel joke on you?

Things get even worse when Paige and Isabel show up with bad news. "We were just at Five-Points Plaza," Isabel says, "and people are talking about Kayla. Becca has been telling everyone that Kayla stole jewelry from our tent."

"What?" you squawk. "How'd that get started?"

Isabel gives you a look, the one that means, *Think about it.* You don't have to, though. You know exactly where those rumors started—with you.

"Well," you say weakly, "she *might* have stolen my bracelet. We still don't know for sure."

Paige shakes her head. "She didn't," she says firmly. "This is the bracelet I saw on Kayla's wrist." She grabs one of the copies off the rack and tosses it on the table in front of you. Your stomach does a somersault.

Turn to page 56.

"Wow," you say to your friends. "I really messed up."

Paige rests a hand on your shoulder. "You just forgot a key rule of kindness," she says. "People are more important than things."

Paige is right. You were so worried about your precious bracelet that you tromped all over Kayla's feelings.

You don't know where your bracelet is, but you know one thing: before you waste any more time trying to find it, you have some apologizing to do. You need to get to Kayla before the rumors reach her, and then you have to do your best to nix those rumors and set things right.

The End

You help Neely gather the last of the spilled beads. "Thanks," she says, blowing a strand of hair off her forehead. "You're a lifesaver."

"No problem," you say. "Those beads are beautiful. I can't wait to see what you make with them!"

You help carry the beads to the jewelry-making table. Neely sits down again at the selling stand, and then you start searching the Market for Emmy.

You weave through a crowd of shoppers, looking for Emmy's long dark hair. You do a full loop of the Market and then another, but there's no sign of Emmy. She's not here, but you have a pretty good idea where she might be. You take off down the path toward Emmy's favorite place: Starfire Lake.

When you reach the boathouse, you spot two girls on the far pier getting into a canoe. That looks like Emmy kneeling on the pier, holding the boat steady. And is that Logan about to step into the canoe? You know that Logan has been wanting to learn how to canoe, and Emmy is the perfect teacher.

Turn to page 80.

You make a quick decision—somebody has to. You tell Neely that you and Olivia will go to dinner with her. Olivia's visit will be over soon, and you know your friends at Innerstar U really want to meet her.

Olivia's reaction to your decision surprises you. She grabs your hand and squeezes it excitedly. "This'll be fun!" she says. Is she putting on a brave face for you, or was she hoping all along to spend time with your new friends? You're not sure.

When you get to the student center, you, Olivia, and Neely meet up with your other friends, including Amber and Shelby, who just got done riding. You can tell by the smiles on your friends' faces that they're all super excited to spend time with Olivia. She seems happy, too, but a little bit nervous. She never did like being the center of attention.

Shelby must notice Olivia's nervousness, too, because she kicks into classic Shelby mode. She invites Olivia to sit by her and then asks a few questions to put Olivia at ease.

"When did you two meet?" Shelby asks. "I mean, how long have you been friends?"

Turn to page 73.

"That's okay," you say to Amber. "I'm starving. Let's eat now and worry about the bracelet later."

You and Amber eat hearty helpings of chicken-noodle casserole, and then you head back to the Market. As you walk toward the donation tents, a girl approaches you carrying a clipboard.

"Hey," she says. "Do you have a minute? I'm taking nominations for the 'volunteer of the day' award."

"The what?" you ask.

Amber quickly explains. "There's a contest going on," she says. "You know, to see who can bring in the most donations or money for the clothing drive."

"Really?" you ask. "Why didn't Isabel mention it?" *I might have found a few more things to donate,* you think, picturing your pathetic offerings from this morning.

"I don't know," says Amber. "Maybe because we're supposed to be doing this out of kindness, not for some grand prize." She gives you a sideways smile.

Oh, right, you think, mentally scolding yourself. But you can't help wondering just what that prize might be . . .

 Turn to page 68.

You loan Olivia riding gear and then walk to the stables, where you find Amber and Shelby trotting around the ring.

"Hi!" says Amber. "Are you guys ready to ride?"

Olivia bites her lip. "I've never ridden a horse before," she says, "but I'd love to try."

"You just need a gentle horse like Angel," says Shelby, patting her quiet palomino.

Shelby helps Olivia mount the horse and leads her around the ring. You ride, too, on a paint horse named Rio.

Both Amber and Shelby are really patient with Olivia and give her lots of pointers. It's a relief for you to see all your friends, old and new, having fun together. You're less worried about everything now, including the lost bracelet.

⭐ Turn to page 67.

Soon you and Olivia are settled at an art table, ready to work on crafts. As you start to string some beads, you notice that Olivia seems awfully quiet.

"Is something wrong?" you ask her.

Olivia hesitates, but she finally tells you the truth. "I feel like you're ashamed of me or something," she says. "Why don't you want me to spend time with your new friends?" Olivia's dark eyes are full of hurt.

"Oh, Livvy," you say, jumping up to put your arm around her. "That's not it! I just didn't want you to feel left out—or to think I'd replaced you as my friend."

Olivia smiles sadly and looks down at her hands. "I *did* worry about that when you first came here," she says. "But now that I'm here with you, it feels like old times. I know you've made a lot of new friends, but our friendship is still just as good as ever, isn't it?"

Olivia's totally right. Being with her today, it's as if no time has passed at all. She's the same old Olivia—and there's no one else quite like her. "We're *great* friends," you reassure her. "And we always will be."

Olivia sighs with relief. "All right then," she says with a smile. "When can I meet these new friends of yours?"

"Right now," you say, reaching for her hand. You're ready to lead Olivia out the door, but she says there's something she has to do first.

Turn to page 72.

It's Olivia who helps you come up with a solution. Actually, it's thinking about how you and Olivia used to keep in touch when you first came to Innerstar U.

Olivia's family had a blog—a website where the family posted updates about their lives. That gets you thinking about websites and how Innerstar U could set one up with a list of all the items at the Lost and Found. Students could just check the website to search for their things. And if an item was posted for a month with no response, the lost item could be donated to Casual Closet's secondhand shop to raise money for charity!

When you get back to the donation tents, you share your idea with Isabel—who just about jumps out of her skin with excitement.

"Let's go ask the student-center staff right away," she says. "It's a great idea. How can they say no?"

As it turns out, they *can't*. Isabel's enthusiasm helps your sales pitch, and the staff gives you the green light!

Turn to page 108.

You push away from the lunch table and walk toward Kayla. When she sees you coming, she smiles. She starts to sit back down, as if she thinks you're going to join her.

You look at the distance between Kayla and the girls at the other end of the table. You suddenly remember what it was like to be the new girl. The anger you had brewing inside you starts to cool.

"Hi," you say. "Mind if I sit down?"

Kayla's smile broadens. As she slides her food tray over, you catch a glimpse of the beads peeking out from beneath her shirtsleeve. Here's your chance.

"Wow, what a pretty bracelet," you say, trying to keep your voice steady.

Kayla glances down at her wrist. "Yeah," she says, pushing back her sleeve. "I just got this today."

Now that you can see the bracelet more clearly, your heart sinks. It's not yours. The cord is a different color.

💙 Turn to page 75.

"Actually," you say, "that one's priceless." You smile and explain to Emmy that the bracelet is yours—a mix-up from this morning.

Emmy looks disappointed. She strokes one of the glass beads for a minute before handing the bracelet back to you. "It's really beautiful," she says.

"It sure is," you agree. As Emmy walks away, you flash back to this morning when you ran to your room to get the bracelet so that you could make others just like it. *There's still plenty of time for that,* you think, checking your watch. Maybe you can make a bracelet like yours for Emmy, plus a few more to sell.

When Neely gets back with more beads and cord, you search her stash for blue glass beads. You find a few pretty ones, which you slide onto cord. You knot the cord just as Olivia did with the bracelet on your own wrist.

When the bracelet is done, Neely loves it. So do other girls who stopped by the table while you were working. You set the bracelet aside for Emmy, and then you make a few more—which sell quickly.

At noon, when it's time to leave the table, you're feeling great. You found your priceless bracelet, and you found a way to "share" it with others, too!

The End

After riding, you all head over to the student center for a snack. You find a table outside on the upper deck, overlooking the water. For a moment, all is right with the world. Then Shelby takes off her riding jacket, and you see what's on her wrist. You freeze.

Shelby is wearing *your* bracelet from Olivia. In fact, Shelby and Olivia are sitting side by side, their matching bracelets nearly touching. You almost choke on a bite of brownie.

Luckily, Olivia is having a lively conversation with Amber about horses. She hasn't looked down, and you hope she won't anytime soon.

 If you say something privately to Shelby about the bracelet, turn to page 78.

 If you keep your mouth closed and hope no one will notice the twin bracelets, turn to page 101.

You don't nominate anyone for the award—until another hour goes by and you see just how hard your friends are working.

Amber had to leave, but Shelby is still sorting clothes. She has moved on to a pile of pants now and shows no signs of slowing down. Neely is still busily making and selling jewelry. And Isabel? She must be on her nineteenth trip to Casual Closet to deliver more clothes.

When you see the girl with the clipboard again, you flag her down.

"I have three friends I'd like to nominate for that award," you say, reaching for her pencil.

"Sorry," says the girl. "You can vote for just one person. Otherwise, this list would be a mile long!"

You pause for a moment, and then you write down a name. Which friend do you nominate?

 If you nominate Isabel, turn to page 76.

If you nominate Shelby, turn to page 95.

If you nominate Neely, turn to page 102.

"Wait, that's mine!" you shout, grabbing the bracelet out of Emmy's hands. She lets go quickly and holds up her hands in the air.

"Um . . . sorry!" she says. "It's not worth fighting over."

Actually, it kind of is, you think to yourself, remembering how you felt when the bracelet was lost. But now you're embarrassed by your outburst.

"Sorry, Emmy," you say. "I didn't mean to be rude. This accidentally got mixed up with my donations. I guess someone found it and put it out on the jewelry table. It's mine—it's not for sale."

"Oh," says Emmy. "Wow. Well, I'm glad you found it. It sure is pretty." She flips through the other jewelry on the rack and chooses a stretchy bracelet with round turquoise beads. She pays for the bracelet and then turns to leave, calling over her shoulder, "Good luck with the clothing drive!"

You thank Emmy, but as she disappears into the crowd, you realize that you've already had a stroke of luck today. If you hadn't agreed to help Neely with the jewelry sale, you might never have found your bracelet. Now that it's back on your wrist, it's time to share your good fortune— by selling more bracelets and raising more money.

But first? Neely needs help of a different kind. You slide off your chair and get down on the ground to help your friend gather up those precious beads.

The End

The next morning, you and Isabel stand at the snack table in the basement of Casual Closet. Your job is to greet people who come in, but so far, there haven't been many. Then you catch sight of a brown-haired girl coming down the stairs, her mother close behind. When you offer them cookies and juice, the girl looks shyly at you, but she takes a cookie from the table. Her blue eyes brighten when she sees all the clothing on the racks in the room beyond.

As the girl begins exploring the room, her mother stays behind to talk with you and Isabel. "We had a fire in our home," the woman explains to you. "We lost everything. It's been really hard on my daughter, Faith."

You're shocked. You didn't realize that some of the girls who would come into this shop would be girls like Faith, who'd lost everything.

When you see Faith flipping through the jeans on the rack, you hurry over and help her find her size. As she tries them on behind the curtain in the back of the room, you and Isabel find a few more things you think might fit Faith. One of them is a T-shirt with an owl on the front.

Faith smiles when she sees the shirt. "Thanks," she says. "I used to have one like that." Her eyes cloud over for just a moment before she flashes another smile at you and ducks behind the curtain.

Turn to page 82.

You watch Olivia work, and pretty soon you catch on to what she's doing: she's making you a new bracelet. The beads are a little different from hers, but the bracelet is every bit as beautiful.

"Wow," you say when Olivia hands you the finished bracelet. "Thank you!"

"You see?" she says. "You shouldn't have worried about losing your bracelet. Bracelets can be replaced."

"Maybe," you say, running your fingers along the beads. "But friendships can't. Each one is pretty special—especially ours. You know that, right?"

Olivia smiles at you and nods. She takes a minute to tie your new bracelet onto your wrist. Then she grabs your hand and squeezes it as she follows you out the door.

The End

It's a funny thing, but when Shelby asks when you and Olivia first met, your mind goes blank. Olivia remembers, though. "It was at summer camp," she says. "We were six."

Olivia grins at you, and suddenly, you can picture exactly how she looked the day you met her. Her knees were muddy beneath her skirt, and she was missing a front tooth. But she invited you right into the circle of friends she was playing with. She had a kind heart. She must have known that you were new to camp and feeling shy.

As Olivia tells the story of the day you met, you feel a warm rush of affection for your friend. Here at Innerstar U, *she's* the new girl, and she must be feeling a little shy—just as you were that first day at camp so long ago. But she *does* want to meet your new friends. She's just been waiting for you to extend the invitation.

After dinner, you extend another invitation: you ask Olivia to come back again soon. Now that you've made some new memories with your friend, you're really going to miss her. And your other friends want Olivia to come back again, too, so that they can get to know her better.

Turn to page 96.

There's no time to waste—you have to find Emmy before she gets too far away with that bracelet. You do a complete loop of the Market. Just as you're about to head to the lake to search for Emmy, you spot Neely walking toward you. She's scowling.

"Where *were* you?" Neely asks, throwing her hands in the air. "You were supposed to be watching the money box!"

Your mouth goes dry. "But . . . you were back," you protest. "Weren't you watching it?"

Neely shakes her head. "I was bringing supplies to the girls making jewelry," she says. "*No one* was watching the money box. And now fifteen dollars is missing."

What? You were gone for just a few minutes. How did this happen?

If you replace the stolen money with your own money, turn to page 85.

If you make bracelets to earn back the money that was lost, turn to page 106.

If you search for the money thief, go online to innerstarU.com/secret and enter this code: UR2KIND

You're incredibly disappointed about the bracelet. Now that you're sitting with Kayla, though, you can't just get up and leave. She's studying your face, probably trying to figure out why your mood just took a nosedive.

You try to think of something friendly to say, but Kayla beats you to it. "Do you want to stop at the bakery to grab something sweet?" she asks. Her eyes are hopeful, but she also looks a little nervous. Again, you flash back to your first few days here at Innerstar U, when you were missing Olivia and hoping to make some new friends.

"Yes," you say. "I'd love to."

As you walk to the bakery, you ask Kayla about her old school. She tells you about the friends she had there, especially her good friend Quinn.

 Turn to page 79.

That's a no-brainer, you think to yourself as you write Isabel's name on the nomination sheet. All of your friends are working hard, but Isabel practically organized the whole clothing drive. Without her, this project never would have happened.

When Isabel's name is announced over the loud-speaker at the end of the day, no one cheers louder than you. Isabel blushes as she steps onto the stage to receive her award.

Isabel's award is a golden heart trophy, which seems fitting. She volunteered her time today out of the goodness of her heart, but that kindness deserves recognition, you think. You snap a picture of Isabel, and then you give her a huge hug—straight from the heart.

The End

"Hey, Shelby," you say, "Can I show you something?"
You lead her to the deck railing and pretend to be pointing
out toward the horse stables. Then you lean in and whisper
in her ear.

"Where did you find that bracelet?" you ask. "It's mine,
from Olivia—I lost it a week ago!"

Shelby's jaw drops. "Really?" she whispers. "I got it at
the Market. It was part of the Care and Share fund-raiser.
I bought it for . . ." Her voice trails off, and she looks away.

"For what?" you ask.

"For you," Shelby finishes. "I bought it for you
because I thought it looked like something you'd love. But
then I started wondering whether I really knew your style."

You giggle at that. "Well, obviously, you *do*!" you say.
"You picked out something for me that was actually mine."

Shelby laughs a little, too, but then her face grows
somber. "Yeah," she says, "but I also gave you a striped
shirt last year, and I saw that you gave it away. Sorry about
that—I guess it wasn't really you."

Your mind starts spinning. Is that what started all
of this? The fact that you never told Shelby you had two
identical striped shirts?

Turn to page 90.

Kayla stops walking so that she can show you the round locket she's wearing around her neck. There are two tiny pictures inside. One looks like her, and the other is of Quinn, a dark-haired girl with a sweet smile.

"I wear it every day," says Kayla.

You nod—you get that. You used to wear your bracelet from Olivia every day, too. Why did you stop wearing it? Maybe because you finally started to feel better—as if you belonged here at Innerstar U. You hope you'll be able to find the bracelet, but if you don't, that's okay, too. You had it when you needed it most.

"It gets easier," you say kindly to Kayla. "You'll make friends here quickly—I can tell."

You offer to give Kayla a tour of your favorite spots on campus. Your friends might miss you back at the Market, but something tells you that spending time with Kayla is the right thing to do. Today is all about being kind to people in need, and Kayla—your new friend—needs *you*.

The End

You have to get the girls' attention before they pull away from the pier. "Emmy!" you shout.

Emmy doesn't hear you, but Logan does. She looks up and waves—then promptly loses her balance. The canoe pushes away from the pier, and Logan sinks into the crack between the two. *Splash!*

Emmy jumps into the water after her. By the time you get there, both girls are soaking wet but giggling. You help them pull the canoe onto shore.

Turn to page 84.

By the time Faith and her mother are ready to leave, they have two brown paper bags full of clothes. Faith's mother talks with Isabel and the owner of Casual Closet while you and Faith carry the bags up the stairs and out to the sidewalk. You want to ask Faith about the fire, but you don't quite know what to say.

"It must be weird, starting over with different clothes," you say to Faith. It's a weak opening, but it's all you can come up with.

Faith nods. "It is," she says. "But I don't miss my old clothes all that much. What I really miss are things like Jackson, the stuffed rabbit I'd had since I was two. And the scrapbooks my friends and I made." Faith's eyes start to fill with tears.

Your stomach clenches. You didn't mean to make her cry. "I'm sorry you lost all those memories," you say quickly, trying to comfort her.

Faith wipes away the tears and shakes her head. "I still have those," she says. "The memories, I mean. I just have to find new ways to hang on to them."

Faith's words make you think of your bracelet, which you may never see again. Suddenly, it seems a lot less important than it did this morning. You didn't lose your memories of your fun times with Olivia. You just need to find new ways to keep them alive.

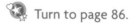 Turn to page 86.

Isabel must be thinking the same thing you are, because her blue eyes brighten. "We should ask Neely about your bracelet," she says excitedly. "She was working at the jewelry stand all morning. Maybe your bracelet got mixed up in the things she was selling!"

You suddenly feel sick. What if someone bought your bracelet? It could be anywhere right now—with anyone.

Paige sees the expression on your face. "Don't give up," she says, squeezing your hand. "Let's go talk to Neely— maybe she knows where the bracelet is."

You and your friends make it to the Market in record time. There's Neely, still sitting beside the jewelry-selling stand. You wonder if she's had a chance to break for lunch, but before you can ask her that, you have to know about your bracelet. As you start to describe it to Neely, you can tell by the look on her face that she has seen it—you're sure of it.

"Yeah, that *did* end up on my table!" Neely says. "And everyone here loved it. It sold right away."

Sold? Uff. The word falls like a boulder in your stomach.

 Turn to page 87.

Now that everyone is back on dry land, you explain to Emmy that you came to the lake hoping to take a peek at the bracelet she bought.

Emmy glances down at her wrist. "This one?" she asks, holding up her arm. And there it is—your bracelet from Olivia. It's wet and a little muddy now, after the last few action-packed minutes, but it's still a beautiful sight.

"That one," you sigh. "I'm sorry, Emmy. It's mine. I don't know how it got mixed up in the jewelry sale."

Emmy bites her lip as she untangles a soggy leaf from the braided cord of the bracelet. "I'm sorry, too," she says. "I got it all wet." She carefully slides the bracelet from her wrist and hands it back to you.

There's an awkward pause. You feel bad about ruining your friends' canoe outing *and* about leaving Emmy without a bracelet, especially since she paid for one.

 If you go to get Emmy's money back, turn to page 100.

 If you tell Emmy you'll make her another bracelet, turn to page 112.

You're so ashamed, you can hardly look at Neely. You can't believe you walked away from the money box without asking anyone to watch over it.

"I have money in my piggy bank," you mumble. "I'll replace what was stolen."

Without waiting for Neely's response, you turn on your heel and start jogging toward Brightstar House. As you pass through Five-Points Plaza, you keep your eyes on the ground. You don't want to see anyone you know or talk to anyone right now. This day has been a total disaster. Not only did you lose your bracelet from Olivia, but you *also* lost the money that your friends worked so hard to raise. Could things get any worse?

 Turn to page 91.

After Faith and her mother leave Casual Closet, you join Isabel back inside the store. You enjoyed meeting Faith, but after hearing her story, you suddenly feel guilty.

"I wish I'd donated more to the clothing drive," you admit to Isabel sadly.

"You volunteered your time," says Isabel. "That's important, too."

Isabel's words make you feel a little better. You still wish, though, that there was more you could do to help Faith. Maybe there *is*.

If you gather more clothes for Faith, turn to page 99.

If you help her hang on to memories, turn to page 88.

Volunteering your time is important, too.

When Neely sees your expression change, her face falls, too. "Oh," she says. "I'm really sorry. But, here, check these out. The girls making jewelry liked your bracelet so much, they made some that are kind of like it." Neely shows you a few bracelets dangling from the rack. They do look a lot like yours, except for the turquoise cords.

Suddenly it clicks—this is where Kayla got her bracelet. You and Paige glance at each other, and she gives you an apologetic smile. She obviously feels guilty about pointing the finger at Kayla. You do, too, but you're relieved that you never actually confronted Kayla.

"Do you remember who bought the original bracelet?" asks Logan, always the detective.

Neely thinks about that. "There were so many girls coming in and out of here," she says. "Wait, was it Shelby? Yeah, it was definitely Shelby. And she was so excited about it. She said it was the perfect gift for a friend."

Shelby? Oh, no. Shelby is one of your favorite people at Innerstar U. She's friends with everybody, so it doesn't surprise you that she bought the bracelet as a gift. You wonder if she has already given it away. And if she hasn't, will you have the heart to take it back from her?

 If you try to figure out which friend Shelby bought the bracelet for, turn to page 89.

 If you ask Shelby for the bracelet back, turn to page 94.

Neely helps you come up with a special gift for Faith: a scrapbook she can fill with memories of good times with friends. While you're at it, you make one for yourself, too.

You decide that starting today, you're going to write down one memory every day of something you did with Olivia. And you'll invite her to Innerstar U sometime soon so that you can make *new* memories, too. You may not find the bracelet Olivia made for you, but you'll never lose touch with her—or your memories of your time together.

The End

You don't know what to do. You need more information, like whether Shelby has already given the bracelet away—and to whom. It looks as if your undercover mission will continue, but at least this time, you have co-agent Logan by your side.

Leaving Isabel and Paige behind at the jewelry tent, you and Logan walk along the path toward Five-Points Plaza.

"We need to make a plan," Logan says, all business as she leads you to a deserted corner of the plaza. The gushing water of the fountain makes it hard to hear. Maybe that's why Logan brought you here.

"I'll try to get Shelby's school schedule," she says. "And then we can take shifts—you know, to follow her and see if she delivers a wrapped package to anyone."

"A 'wrapped package'? Logan, you've been reading too many spy novels," you say, giggling. "I have a better plan: Why don't we just ask Shelby about the bracelet? We can say that Neely told us about a beautiful bracelet that Shelby bought as a gift. Maybe she'll show it to us or tell us who it's for."

Logan looks crushed. "That's way too easy," she says with a sigh. "But . . . okay."

Turn to page 92.

"Sheesh, Shelby," you say. "I love that striped shirt! In fact, I loved it so much that I bought one for myself, not knowing you'd gotten one for me. I didn't tell you I had two of them because I didn't want to hurt your feelings."

That sounds ridiculous now. After all, it was because you weren't honest with Shelby that you *did* hurt her feelings. If you'd told her the truth from the beginning, everything would have been okay.

Shelby smiles with relief. She glances back at Olivia and Amber, who have stopped talking about horses and have moved on to ponies. Then Shelby slips the bracelet off her wrist. "Here," she whispers. "This is yours. I'm sorry I didn't give it to you sooner."

You slide the bracelet onto your own wrist, and then you give Shelby a hug. "Thank you," you whisper. "Thanks for being such a great friend."

Shelby really *has* become a great friend to you. She knows what you like and don't like, and she goes out of her way to be kind to you. As you watch Shelby sit back down next to Olivia, you wonder, *Is it possible to have more than one best friend?* Seeing Olivia talking with Amber—her new friend—makes you think that maybe it is.

Sitting in the middle of that circle of friends, you make a decision: you'll invite Olivia back to Innerstar U often. The only thing better than hanging out with your old best friend is hanging out with *all* of your friends, together.

The End

When you get back to your room, you take a minute to look in the mirror and give yourself a good talking-to. You think back to the start of the day, when you were trying to get some things together for the Care and Share clothing drive. *Caring and sharing.* You sure haven't done much of either today. For the rest of the day, you decide, you'll try harder.

As for your bracelet? You'll track down Emmy later and figure it out. You've put enough time—and now money— toward that today. You sigh as you shake the money out of your piggy bank and onto your bed. You count out fifteen dollars, tuck it into your pocket, and head for the door.

The End

Shelby isn't hard to track down. She's in the yearbook office at the student center, where she's editing some video footage she took of the Care and Share clothing drive.

Shelby opens the door humming, clearly in a good mood. It takes about two seconds for you and Logan to spot the "wrapped package" sitting on the desk behind her. It's a small, square box wrapped in green-and-white-striped paper. It has to be the bracelet.

"Wow," says Logan as she walks into the office. "Pretty package. Who's it for?" She sure doesn't waste any time getting down to business!

Shelby dances toward the desk, picks up the gift, and hides it behind her back. "It's a surprise," she says, her dark eyes twinkling. "But you're all going to love it."

All? How many people is she giving the bracelet to? You picture a bunch of your friends fighting over the bracelet—until the cord breaks and beads spill across the floor.

Shelby slides something else off the desk. "Here," she says. "I was going to deliver these to your rooms, but you saved me a trip."

Shelby hands you and Logan two party invitations. "I thought we could have a picnic in the meadow at noon tomorrow," she says. "We deserve to have some fun after the big clothing drive today. Can you come?"

Turn to page 98.

You find Shelby in her room after dinner. When she sees the troubled look on your face, she furrows her brow, that little sign that says she's all ears. "What is it?" she asks.

You tell Shelby the whole story—how Olivia made the bracelet for you, how it accidentally ended up on the sales table, and how you're really hoping to get it back from Shelby. You expect her to be disappointed. Instead, she starts giggling.

"What?" you ask her. "What's so funny?"

Shelby pulls open a desk drawer and picks up a small box. She takes off the lid and hands the box to you. Tucked inside is your beautiful bracelet.

"I bought it for *you*," Shelby says. "I took one look at it and knew it was something you'd love. Now I know why I was so sure about that." She giggles again.

Wow. Shelby's amazing. She knows just what you like, and she's so generous. She's always looking out for other people's feelings and trying to make them feel good. *You could have done a better job of that today,* you realize, thinking of Kayla.

This bracelet is pretty amazing, too. It was given to you now by not one good friend, but *two*. You tie the bracelet around your wrist. It still reminds you of Olivia, but now it reminds you of something else—the generosity that Shelby showed you, and the kindness that you need to pass on to others, too.

The End

You write down Shelby's name. Why? Because Shelby is a kind, giving person *every* day of the year, not just on Care and Share Day.

Shelby doesn't win the "volunteer of the day" award. It goes to Isabel, which also feels right. But you make a point of telling Shelby that if there were a "volunteer of the year" award, you're sure she would win it.

"Aw, thanks," says Shelby, smiling sweetly. Then she tells you that she has a "reward" for you, too, for working all day at the donation tents. She pulls something out of her pocket and tucks it into your hand. You feel what it is before you can see it—it's a beaded bracelet.

 Turn to page 104.

You really *do* miss Olivia after she leaves. It helps that when you open your mailbox at the student center a few days later, you find a package from Olivia tucked inside. You don't open it right away. You wait until you're back in your room, sitting on the edge of your bed. Then you carefully open the thick brown envelope and shake the contents onto your bedspread.

The first thing that falls out is a beautiful new bracelet. This one is made with different-colored beads: magenta, emerald green, gold, and rose. And right in the middle? There's a bright blue bead, like the one on the first bracelet that Olivia made for you.

There's a note in the envelope, too. It says, "Every bead is unique, just like each of your new friends. It was great to meet them—and to see you! Love, your true-blue friend, Olivia."

There's one more thing in the envelope: a photo of you and Olivia sitting at the dinner table with all of your Innerstar U friends. You remember taking the photo with Olivia's camera just before dinner. Seeing the smiling faces in that photo makes *you* smile, too.

You tie the bracelet onto your wrist right away. You don't think you'll be taking it off anytime soon. Then you put the photo where it belongs—taped to your vanity mirror, front and center, surrounded by pictures of all the friends who mean the most to you.

The End

"Of course we'll be there," you tell Shelby.

"Yay! I'm going to run to Brightstar House to deliver the rest of these," she says, picking up a stack of invitations. She sets the wrapped gift down on the desk while she saves a file on the computer. Then she hops up from the chair and heads for the door, leaving the gift behind.

"Are you guys coming?" Shelby calls as she reaches for the doorknob. You hesitate. Logan is gesturing wildly from behind Shelby's back. She obviously wants you to stay here to get a closer look at the gift, but you don't know how you can pull that off without Shelby questioning you.

⭐ If you try to stay behind to examine the gift, turn to page 105.

⭐ If you leave the student center with Shelby and Logan, turn to page 107.

You spend the rest of your time at Casual Closet trying to picture the clothes in your *own* closet. Is there something in there that you can give to Faith? She's smaller than you, so most of what you own won't fit her. Then it hits you— the perfect thing!

When your shift at the store is over, you can hardly wait to get back to your room. You head straight for your closet. You pull the rhinestone-studded jeans from the hanger and check the tag inside. You squeal. They're Faith's size, just as you'd hoped they would be! You think she'll really like them. If you bring the jeans to Casual Closet, maybe the owner can find a way to get them to Faith.

On your way out of your closet, you grab something from your jewelry box, too: a porcelain owl pin. You pin it to the front pocket of the jeans, a little something special to make Faith smile.

You know that the jeans themselves aren't important— Faith told you that. But she also showed you what *is* important: generosity among friends, old and new.

The End

"I'll get your money back," you tell Emmy.

You head toward the Market, but something makes you change direction and walk to Brightstar House instead. This was *your* mix-up. You spent more time this morning worrying about your own possessions than you did about donating to others. If you need to pull cash out of a money box, it should be from your own piggy bank, not Neely's cash box at the jewelry-selling stand.

When you get back to your room, you shake out coins from your piggy bank. You count out two dollars, plus a few extra dollars, too—a donation for the Care and Share fund-raiser. Your piggy bank hasn't been this empty in a long time, but your hands and heart are full.

The End

You're sweating now. You have no idea how Shelby got your bracelet, but if Olivia sees it, she's going to think you gave it to Shelby. What are you going to do?

You have to think fast. You glance around and see Shelby's riding jacket hanging on the back of her chair. "Hey, Shelby," you say. "That's a great jacket. Can you put it on again so that I can see how it zips up the front?"

Shelby happily obliges. That buys you a few seconds of relief before Shelby peels the jacket off again. "It's really warm out here in the sun," she says.

"It sure feels good, though, doesn't it?" Olivia asks, stretching out her arms to catch a few rays. And that does it. Shelby spots the bracelet on Olivia's wrist.

 Turn to page 103.

It's a tough choice, but you end up nominating Neely for the volunteer award. All of your friends are working hard, but Neely is the most enthusiastic. You can tell that she loves making jewelry, and because of that, she's a great salesperson, too. Her cash box is already full of money, which will help a lot of people.

Neely doesn't win the "volunteer of the day" award—that goes to Isabel. As Isabel accepts her golden heart trophy, you lean over and whisper to Neely that you think she should have received the "golden smile" award.

"Thanks," she says, flashing you that smile. And then she's off again, finding some other way to turn her passion for crafts into cash—for a good cause.

The End

"Hey, check it out!" Shelby says. "We have the same bracelet!" She holds her wrist next to Olivia's. Olivia does a double-take, and then she glances at you, confusion clouding her brown eyes.

You don't know what to say. You're confused, too, but now you have no choice but to speak up. "Where did you get that?" you ask Shelby. "Olivia made one just like it for me, and I lost it somewhere."

Olivia glances from you to Shelby and back again. From the look on her face, you're not sure whether she believes that you lost the bracelet. She probably thinks you gave it to Shelby and are lying now to cover your tracks. You wish you had just been honest with her from the start.

Then Shelby speaks up—and solves the mystery. "I bought it at the Market," she says. "From Neely's jewelry stand. I thought she had made it. I'm sorry!"

Shelby tries to take the bracelet off her wrist, but it gets stuck. The cord suddenly breaks, and a bead bounces off the table. "Oh!" says Shelby. She holds up the broken bracelet, staring at it in shock.

🌀 Turn to page 110.

In fact, it's not just any old bracelet—it's *your* bracelet from Olivia. "My bracelet!" you gasp. "Where did you find it?"

"Huh?" says Shelby, equally surprised. "It's yours? But I bought it from Neely's jewelry table!"

It takes you and Shelby some time and brain power to sort it all out. Somehow your bracelet got mixed up in the things you donated to the clothing drive, got mixed up in the jewelry that Neely was selling, and then miraculously ended up being the very piece of jewelry that Shelby bought for you.

"I'm sorry that you had to pay for something that was already mine," you say to Shelby, but she just laughs.

"It was for a good cause," she says. That's Shelby for you—always generous and kind. You're grateful for her gift, and even more grateful for her friendship.

The End

You walk out of the office with Shelby and Logan, but halfway down the hall, you stop.

"Hey, wait up," you say. "I just remembered that I left my water bottle in the lunchroom."

Shelby's face brightens. "I'll go back with you," she says. "I want to ask the kitchen staff if they can help us with the picnic lunch tomorrow."

You're sure that your less-than-perfect plan is ruined until Logan jumps in to save the day. "Shelby, you can do that later," she says. "The most important thing is to get these invitations out. Who cares about food if you don't have any *guests* at your picnic?"

That logic works for Shelby. She lets Logan hurry her down the hall and out the front door of the student center. When they're out of sight, you run back into the yearbook office. You pick up the gift and flip over the gift tag. There's a name written in Shelby's handwriting: *Kayla*.

Turn to page 109.

You immediately do some mental math. Fifteen dollars? That's about seven or eight bracelets. You promise Neely that you'll sit down right away and make eight bracelets. "And then," you tell her, "I'll stay at the jewelry-selling stand until I've sold every last one of them."

Neely's expression softens. "I'll help," she says. "We'll do it together."

By working together, you and Neely quickly make up the money you lost. Plus, you have the chance to explain to Neely why you left the table in such a hurry.

"I'm sorry about your bracelet," Neely says. "I'll help you track it down later—I promise."

By the end of the day, you've accomplished so much and had such a good time with Neely that you've almost forgotten about your bracelet—almost. But when you hear a knock on your door and see Emmy standing there, holding your bracelet, you're thrilled.

"Neely said this might belong to you," Emmy says sweetly. "Sorry about the mix-up."

It's great to have your bracelet back, but you feel even better knowing that you used the lost bracelet as inspiration to make and sell many more. Now the bracelet not only reminds you of Olivia, but it reminds you of a great day of caring and sharing, too.

The End

You can't think up a good excuse for staying behind in the yearbook office. You're just no good at this snooping-around thing. Logan looks exasperated. She decides to take matters into her own hands.

As you and Shelby begin walking toward the front door of the student center, Logan says that she needs to hang back for a bit. "I want to check my hours at the bakery," she says, "and maybe tidy up some things from this morning."

Shelby shrugs and waves good-bye to Logan, and you give Logan a hidden thumbs-up. Then you walk Shelby back to Brightstar House. She chatters all the way about the picnic. As you cross the footbridge just before Brightstar House, Shelby pulls you over to the railing.

"Can you keep a secret?" she asks you, her eyes shining.

"Um, yeah, definitely," you say. You've kind of proven that today, for better or for worse.

Shelby goes on to tell you that the picnic is really for Kayla—a way to welcome her to Innerstar U. "That gift you saw," says Shelby, "was a surprise for her. It's something I know she's going to love."

For Kayla? you think. *You're giving my bracelet to someone we don't even know?* It feels like a punch in the stomach.

Shelby doesn't seem to notice the pained look on your face. She's too excited. "I had to tell someone," she says, tugging your hand to get you moving along the path again. "Thanks for listening!"

 Turn to page 113.

It takes a few weeks for the Lost and Found website to get up and running, but when it does, it's a success. Your friend Riley finds one of her lost sweatshirts on the site. Another friend, Logan, finds her book on constellations—a book that she was sure had disappeared into a black hole.

Your bracelet never turns up on the website, but that's okay. You helped return plenty of other things to their owners, and you found a great way to donate clothing and raise money for charity, too!

The End

You can't believe it. Of all the friends Shelby has here on campus, she's giving your bracelet to *Kayla*, a girl she barely knows? You don't know whether to laugh or cry.

The longer you think about it, though, the more sense it makes. Shelby is the girl who always reaches out to new people. She was the first student who introduced herself to you when you were new at Innerstar U. Of course she's being sweet to Kayla. Why wouldn't she be?

You could stand to be a little kinder to Kayla, too. You think about the way you treated her earlier today when you thought she had stolen your bracelet. You hang your head, feeling shame and sadness all mixed into one. You need to be kinder to Kayla. But does that really mean letting her have the bracelet that Olivia made for you?

 If you decide to let Shelby give the bracelet to Kayla, turn to page 114.

 If you talk to Shelby and tell her the bracelet is yours, turn to page 111.

Olivia jumps right in to make things better. You'd forgotten how calm and kind she was during times like this.

"Don't worry about it, Shelby," she says. "I can fix that!"

Olivia finds the bead under the table. Then she takes the bracelet from Shelby. First, Olivia tries to tie the two frayed ends of the cord back together. When that doesn't work, she starts untying the knots in the cord.

Shelby looks horrified. "What are you doing?" she asks.

You're a little worried, too, but you know how creative Olivia can be. She has a plan. She slides the beads off the cord, and then she unravels the cord into three strands. She uses each strand to make a new bracelet: one for you, one for Shelby, and one for Amber.

"See?" Olivia says, holding up the three bracelets. "It's all good." Shelby looks hugely relieved—and pretty excited to have a handmade bracelet of her own.

Wearing your sort-of-matching bracelets makes you, Olivia, Shelby, and Amber seem closer somehow. You were worried that your lost bracelet would hurt Olivia's feelings. As it turns out, it brought you and your friend—you and *all* your friends—closer together.

Friendship is kind of like that bracelet, you decide. It's strong enough to survive change—and definitely meant to be shared.

The End

You carry the gift all the way back to Brightstar House. You find Shelby in her room with Logan, planning for the picnic. When Shelby sees the gift in your hands, she scrunches up her brow. "What are you doing with that?" she asks.

"Long story," you sigh. You glance at Logan. "Do you mind if Shelby and I talk for a minute?" you ask her.

Logan jumps up quickly and excuses herself. You're grateful for that. You know it must be killing Logan, wondering whom the gift is for, but you have to talk with Shelby before you let this go on any further.

Logan leaves and shuts the door behind her, and then you turn back to Shelby's sweet face. You really hate disappointing her this way, but then you picture Olivia's face—and how she would feel if she knew you were "giving away" the bracelet she made especially for you. That image gives you the courage to say what you have to say to Shelby.

"I know this is for Kayla," you begin. "But I can't let you give it to her. It's mine."

 Turn to page 116.

"You know, Emmy," you say, "I saw the beads Neely brought back to the Market with her. There are some swirly ones that remind me of ocean waves. You'd *love* them. How about if I make you a new bracelet?"

Emmy perks right up. "Thanks!" she says. "That's really nice of you."

You hurry back along the path toward the Market. Along the way, you glance down at your bracelet. It looks a little pathetic now, all wet and tangled up in the palm of your hand. The beads are beautiful, it's true, but you know now that what makes your bracelet special isn't the blue beads or the way Olivia braided the cord. It's that Olivia made the bracelet *just for you*.

Emmy liked your bracelet a lot—you could tell. But she's going to love the one you make, too, because it'll be made just for her—a special bracelet for a special friend.

The End

Shelby leaves you at the door to your room so that she can finish delivering invitations. You slump down on your bed, wondering what to do now. At least you solved the mystery. But now that you know your bracelet is going to a stranger, you're not sure if you feel better or worse.

You think of Olivia. Suddenly, you can't picture her face. That scares you. Are you forgetting her now that you don't have the bracelet to remind you?

You step into your closet and slide a shoe box off the shelf. It's full of letters and cards from Olivia. You pour them out on your rug and start reading them, one by one.

One card says "Good luck!" on the front in Olivia's loopy handwriting. Inside, it's her wishes for your new school year at Innerstar U. "Make new friends," she says, "but don't forget to write to me so that I can hear all about them! Love, Livvy." At the bottom is a P.S.: "I made this bracelet for you. Wear it when you need to feel brave."

Turn to page 117.

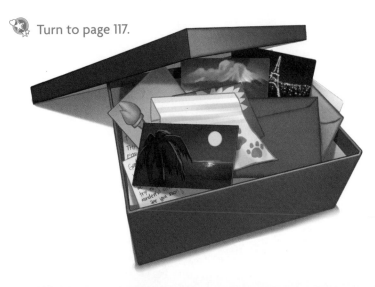

Something stops you from telling Shelby that the bracelet is yours. Maybe it's guilt. Maybe it's remembering what it was like to be the new girl. When Logan asks you later if you found out who the gift is for, you say you're not sure.

The next day, you walk with Logan to Morningstar Meadow. Shelby is already there, smoothing out a picnic blanket and helping the kitchen crew unpack sandwiches from a cooler.

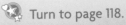

When the other girls arrive, Shelby announces that she's having the picnic to welcome a new girl to Innerstar U. Standing beside Shelby, Kayla looks so nervous, she can barely take her eyes off the ground. Suddenly, you don't mind a bit that this girl will be wearing your friendship bracelet. Maybe she needs it more than you do right now.

Turn to page 118.

"Huh?" Shelby asks. She takes the gift out of your hands and unwraps it. Then she shows you what's inside: a tiny photo album filled with pictures of you and your friends.

"It's a 'welcome to Innerstar U' gift," Shelby explains. "How is that yours? I mean, your photo is in it, but . . ."

You groan and drop your face in your hands. *Serves me right*, you tell yourself, *for snooping around where I didn't belong.*

"I'm sorry, Shelby," you mumble. "I made a huge mistake. That's a really great gift. Kayla will love it."

Shelby smiles and shakes her head at you. "Thanks," she says. "Maybe now you can help me rewrap it." She hands the gift to you, along with a roll of wrapping paper from behind her desk.

"You've got it," you say. You set to work wrapping the gift. You'll ask Shelby about your bracelet later, after the picnic. Right now it's time to focus on someone else— and something else—for a change. You smooth out a

few creases in the wrapping paper. You want the gift to look perfect for Kayla. She deserves that.

The End

You hold Olivia's card close to your chest. You wish you could see the bracelet right now, but it's all wrapped up and going to someone else—someone who maybe needs it, and the courage that it brings, a little more than you do. It's hard to let go, but something feels right about all of this.

When Logan knocks on your door, all out of breath and ready to tell you what she learned about the gift, you hold up your hand to stop her. "It's okay," you say. "Abort mission. I know the bracelet is for Kayla."

Logan's jaw drops. "How'd you know?" she asks.

"Shelby told me," you say. "And I think it's something Kayla will really like—and really needs."

Logan doesn't know what to say to that. She looks at you with some kind of awe, you think, but she says nothing.

The next day, you and Logan walk together to the meadow. Shelby has all the food arranged on a checkered blanket. When the girls are seated around the blanket, Shelby stands up and announces the real reason for the party: welcoming Kayla to Innerstar U. Kayla stands up and everyone applauds—you, loudest of all.

🌟 Turn to page 118.

When Kayla opens the gift from Shelby, though, you're in for a shock. Instead of the bracelet, Kayla holds up a mini photo album. *Huh?*

Kayla passes the album around. When it gets to you, you see that it's full of photos Shelby took of you and your friends. She wrote your names beside your pictures so that Kayla could get to know you. And there are blank pages at the end. The first one has a note written on it that says, "With room for more fun memories, made with you."

The album is a great gift, but where's your bracelet?

At the end of the picnic, Shelby pulls you aside. She hands you a small box wrapped in the same striped paper as Kayla's gift. "Open it," Shelby says, grinning from ear to ear.

You do, and there, beneath the lid of that box, is your bracelet. You immediately start to cry.

Shelby throws her arm around you. "What is it?" she asks. "Don't you like it? It reminded me so much of you, I had to get it for you."

That makes you laugh, so now you're crying and laughing all at the same time. "It sh-should remind you of m-me," you say. "It's mine!"

Shelby doesn't get it, at least not until you can calm down and explain it to her. Then she thinks it's every bit as funny—and wonderful—as you do.

Later, when the bracelet is back on your wrist, you tell Shelby how much you admire her. "You're always reaching out to help other people," you say to her.

"So are you," Shelby says.

But you know that's not true. Instead of helping your friends at the donation tents yesterday, you spent most of the day tracking down one of your own possessions.

You glance up at Kayla, who is looking through her new photo album. Just a short while ago, you were willing to give up something you loved to help her feel better. So maybe you did *one* nice thing, but Kayla will never know.

"Shelby," you ask, "does a kindness count if no one ever sees it?"

"Sure," Shelby says. "Sometimes *those* are the ones that count the most."

That makes you smile. Your friend has taught you a lot about kindness and friendship, and somehow, your crazy hunt for your missing bracelet did, too.

The End

The kindnesses no one sees may be the ones that count the most.

confident

LOYaL

KiND

faîr